LIZZY'S DO'S AND DON'TS

By Jessica Harper · Illustrated by Lindsay Harper duPont

HarperCollinsPublishers

For Elizabeth and Nora
♥ J.H.

For Sammy, Rosie, and George
♥ L.H.dP.

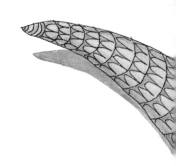

IT SEEMED
TO
LIZZY, ALL
HER MOTHER
EVER SAID
WAS
DON'T!

Don't shout indoors.
Don't tickle so hard.

Don't leave your party shoes
in the yard.

Don't take the deck
and lose one card.

Don't, don't, don't!

Don't climb in trees containing bees.

Don't put 10 Band-Aids on your knees.

Don't cut your hair.

Don't argue, please.

Don't try to reach what's out of reach.

Don't bring the sand home
from the beach.

Don't feed the kitty cat
a peach.

Don't, don't, don't!

Don't hold your breath

'til

you

turn

BLUE.

Don't lick the dog,
though he licks you.

Don't keep that lizard in my shoe!

DON'T

don't

don't!

"Okay, okay, okay, okay,"
said Lizzy. "It's MY turn!"

DON'T

say I can't do so much stuff.

DON'T

huff and puff.

DON'T
say **2** chocolates are enough!

DON'T
act too tough.

Don't, **don't, don't!**

Don't make me wear
that yellow dress.

Don't always say my
hair's a mess.

Don't say no when
you could say yes.
Don't, don't, don't!

Don't hide my candy
up so high.

Don't put nuts
in the apple pie.

When I ask why,
don't frown
and sigh.

Don't
don't
don't!

Don't say to me,
"You should have known."

Don't **chat, chat, chat** on the telephone.

DON'T LICK SO MUCH OF MY ICE-CREAM CONE.

Don't, don't, don't!

"Okay, okay, okay, okay, okay, okay, okay!"
Said Lizzy's Mom,

"The word *don't*
is a tiresome thing to say!"

They thought about it
for a little while,
then Lizzy said . . .

DO teach me how to be prepared.

DO hold me close
when I am scared.

DO take my bike to
get repaired.
Do, do, do!

DO

help me dress up
like a wizard.

DO take me sledding
in a blizzard.

DO please let me keep
the lizard.

do do do do do do do do do do do do do do do do do do do
do do do do do do do do do do do do do do do do do do do
do do do do do do do do do do do do do do do do do do do
do do do do do do do do do do do do do do do do do do do
do do do do do do do do do do do do do do do do do do do
do do do do do do do do do do do do do do do do do do do
do do do do do do do do do do do do do do do do do do do
do do do do do do do do do do do do do do do do do do do
do do do do do do do do do do do do do do do do do do do
do do do do do do do do do do do do do do do do do do do
do do do do do do do do do do do do do do do do do do do
do do do do do do do do do do do do do do do do do do do
do do do do do do do do do do do do do do do do do do do
do do do do do do do do do do do do do do do do do do do
do do do do do do do do do do do do do do do do do do do
do do do do do do do do do do do do do do do do do do do
do do do do do do do do do do do do do do do do do do do
do do do do do do do do do do do do do do do do do do do
do do do do do do do do do do do do do do do do do do do
do do do do do do do do do do do do do do do do do do do
do do do do do do do do do do do do do do do do do do do
do do do do do do do do do do do do do do do do do do do
do do do do do do do do do do do do do do do do do do do
do do do do do do do do do do do do do do do do do do do
do do do do do do do do do do do do do do do do do do do
do do do do do do do do do do do do do do do dodo do do do do do do

𝒟𝑜
𝑑𝑜
𝑑𝑜!

Do tell a fairy tale to me.
Do rock me gently on your knee.
Do, because . . .

Yes, I do, do, do!

Then Lizzy's mother smiled and said,
"Okay, now it's my turn."

Do climb a tree as high as you dare.

Do put some daisies
in your hair.

Do tell me when
life seems unfair.

DO, DO, DO!

DO please be

glad
or

mad
or

sad.

Do wear pink polka dots with plaid.

Do tell some secrets to your dad.

Do, do, do!

Do help me zipper up my dress.
Do tell me if my hair's a mess.
Do ask me if I love you. . . .

I do, DO, DO!